FIFTEEN POUNDS OF MUSCLE AND BOUNCE

Harriet Cole

Illustrated by C.S. Fritz

The Small-Tooth-Dog Publishing Group
P.O. Box 392
Tolleson, Arizona 85353
USA
staff@smalltoothdog.com

ISBN: 9781947408234
Library of Congress Control Number: 2020951796

To the grandkids who listen to my stories.

TABLE OF CONTENTS

A TALE OF A TAIL

IF YOU HAVE EVER BEEN LUCKY ENOUGH TO SEE the north end of a southbound bear, you will have noticed that bears have truly short and stumpy tails. It was not always thus.

There was a time when Bear had the biggest, longest, fluffiest tail in the entire forest. Bear was exceedingly proud of his tail. He thought that tail gave him the right to be the boss of everybody he met.

One day Fox – who had a pretty splendid tail of his own – stole a string of fish out of the stream. Somebody else had caught those fish, but they were his now, and he was going to have a nice lunch!

However, he ran right into Bear, who looked down at him and said, "Where did you get those fish?"

Fox did some quick thinking. He did not want to tell Bear he had stolen the fish because Bear would take them away from him. He couldn't just run away. Bear was too quick. Then he had an idea!

He calmly replied, "I caught them."

Bear asked, "And exactly *how* does a Fox catch fish?"

"With this." Fox waved his fluffy tail at Bear. "It's easy."

Bear had never heard of such a thing. He asked, "Could *I* do that?"

"Follow me." Fox led Bear up into the mountains. Soon they came to a lake that was covered with ice.

"Here," Fox said. "Dig a hole in the ice with your claws and make it just a little bit bigger around than your tail. Then turn around and sit down very carefully so that your tail goes through the ice into the water."

"How is that going to catch fish?"

"Fish love to hide in tail hair," Fox explained. "Your big beautiful tail is going to attract lots and lots of fish – many more than I have. Just sit there all night so the fish have plenty of time to get tangled up in your tail. It'll feel kind of weird and tingly, but you just leave that tail of yours in the water until the sun comes up."

As soon as Bear sat down with his tail in the water, Fox said, "Bye now," picked up his fish and ran away.

Bear sat there all afternoon. Fox was right, it did feel weird, but Bear knew that tingly feeling meant he was going to have lots and lots of fish.

Bear sat there all night. It was freezing and the tingly feeling stopped, but Bear knew that meant there were so many fish in his tail that there wasn't room for any more.

At last the sun came up.

Bear tried to stand up.

He was stuck. He pulled and he twisted. He twisted and he pulled. He began to be afraid all the fish would escape from his tail. He bent and pulled some more and began to be worried that he would never get out of the ice.

So, he twisted and pulled as hard as he could.

As he stood up there was an icy crack which made a loud BOOM! Something did not feel right. Something about his tail felt WRONG.

He looked over his right shoulder and could not see his tail.

He looked over his left shoulder and could not see his tail.

He reached back with his right paw and could not feel his tail.

He reached back with his left paw and could not feel his tail.

Then he realized: He did not have a tail! There was only a stumpy bump where his tail had once been.

Ever since then, bears have had those tiny tails.

Because the bear lost his tail, foxes now have the most beautiful tails in the whole forest.

Maybe this is what Fox wanted after all?

CAT WHO WANTED
TO EAT
THE WHOLE WORLD

ONE MORNING AN OLD WOMAN WHO LIVED
all by herself, except for her big orange cat,
cooked up a kettle of porridge. She added a
nice big herring and then ladled out a bowl for the cat.

"I am going to market," she told him. "The herring
and porridge that is still in the kettle is mine. I will eat
it when I get home."

She picked up her market basket and walked out
the door.

The cat waited. And waited.

He waited some more. And some more.

He waited until it was forever.

He waited until he was starving to death.

The old woman did not come back.

It probably wasn't that long to wait, but you know
how cats are.

He jumped up on the stove. He sniffed the porridge and herring. It smelled wonderful. He took one little bite. And then another.

Then he ate it all.

He ate the old woman's porridge.

He ate her herring.

He ate the kettle and the ladle too!

When the old woman returned, she looked at the stove and she looked at the cat.

"That's a big belly you have there, cat."

"Oh yes," the cat replied.

"I ate my herring,

I ate your herring.

I ate my porridge, I ate your porridge.

I ate the kettle. I ate the ladle. Now . . .

I am going to eat you, too."

The cat opened his mouth so wide that his whiskers stood straight out and his eyes closed. Chomp! Gulp! He swallowed that old woman.

Then he decided to go for a walk, down the street with his striped belly swinging from side to side. "I want to eat the whole world," he said to himself. "I am going to eat the whole world."

Soon he met a man plowing a field with a team of horses pulling the plow. The man looked at him.

"That's a big belly you have there, cat."

"Oh yes," the cat replied.

"I ate my herring.

I ate the old woman's herring.

I ate my porridge. I ate the old woman's porridge.
I ate the kettle. I ate the ladle.
I ate the old woman. Now . . .
I am going to eat you, too."

The cat opened his mouth so wide that his whiskers stood straight out and his eyes closed. Chomp! Gulp! He swallowed the man, the horses, and the plow.

The cat continued his walk down the street with his striped belly swinging from side to side. "I want to eat the whole world," he said. "I am going to eat the whole world."

Soon he met a man planting seeds. The man looked at the beast and said, "That's a big belly you have there, cat."

"Oh yes," the cat replied.

"I ate my herring.
I ate the old woman's herring.
I ate my porridge. I ate the old woman's porridge.
I ate the kettle. I ate the ladle.
I ate the old woman. I ate the plowman.
I ate the horses. I ate the plow. Now . . .
I am going to eat you, too."

The cat opened his mouth so wide that his whiskers stood straight out and his eyes closed. Chomp! Gulp! He swallowed the man, the seed bag, and the seeds.

Then he continued his walk down the street with his striped belly swinging from side to side. "I want to eat the whole world," he said. "I am going to eat the whole world."

Soon he met a woman harvesting hay. The woman looked at him.

"That's a big belly you have there, cat."

"Oh yes," the cat replied.

"I ate my herring.

I ate the old woman's herring.

I ate my porridge. I ate the old woman's porridge.

I ate the ladle. I ate the kettle.

I ate the old woman. I ate the plowman.

I ate the horses. I ate the plow.

I ate the seed man.

I ate the seed bag. I ate the seeds. Now ...

I am going to eat you, too."

The cat opened his mouth so wide that his whiskers stood out and his eyes closed.

But the woman in the hay swung her big harvesting knife at the cat.

Slash! Off went the cat's head.

Crash! Out came the seeds, the seed bag, and the seed man.

Crash!! Out came the plowman, the horses, and the plow.

Dash! The seed man ran away. The plowman ran away. The horses ran away.

Crash! Out came the ladle, the kettle, and the old woman who made the porridge.

"Thank you," she said to the woman in the hay.

The cat's owner dragged the cat's body and head back home. Then she took her sewing kit out of the pocket of her apron, threaded a needle, and sewed the cat's head back on.

And he was as good as new because he was her cat.

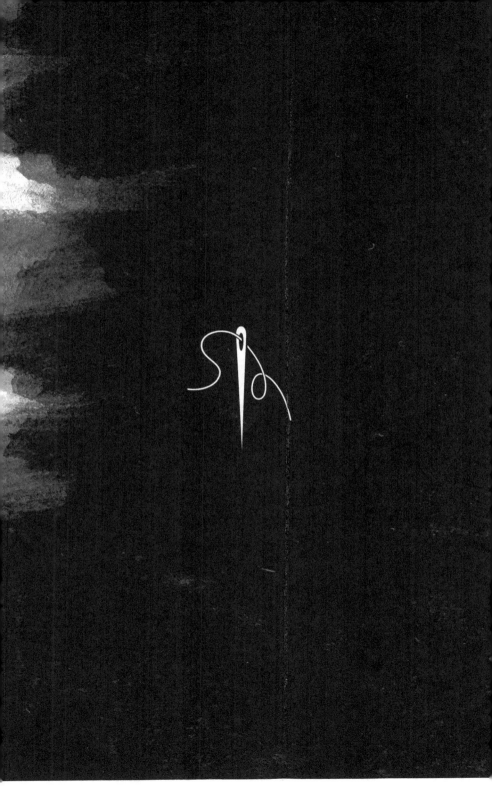

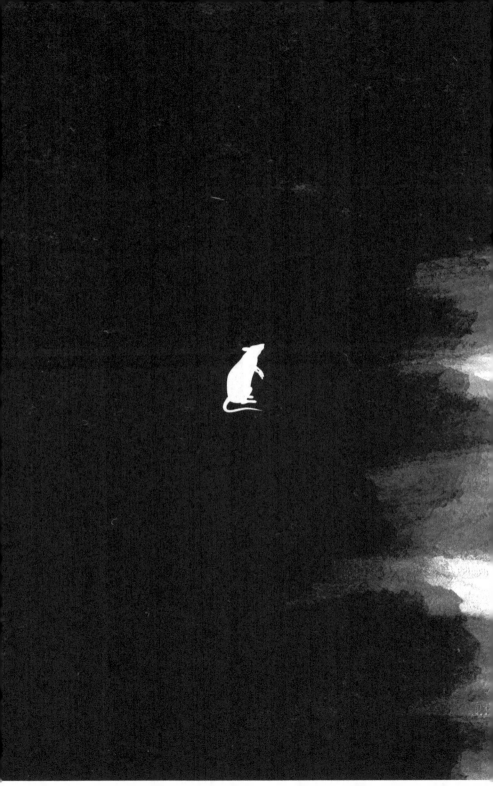

COTTAGER
AND
CAT

A YOUNG MAN AND HIS PARENTS LIVED IN a hut that was little better than a pigsty. Their clothes were nothing but rags.

The young man helped the fishermen unload their boats, just to get a few fish for his poor parents to eat. He helped in the fields, just for a few handfuls of grain that his mother made into a thin porridge. Such young men who labored in the field were sometimes called "cottagers."

His hut and life had always been that way. As far as the young man knew, it would always be that way. But then he had a dream, a *strange* but not *good* dream.

In this dream, a voice said: "Your father will soon die. So will your mother."

This surprised the young man. His parents were old and hungry, but they were not sick.

The voice in the dream continued: "After your parents' funerals, look under their bed. You will find a box."

That was ridiculous. If there was a box under his parents' bed, the young man would already know about it.

"When you open that box, you will find a huge treasure."

The young man decided that this dream was getting silly. If there was a box of treasure under his parents' bed, they wouldn't be nearly starving to death.

"Your father was a thief. Give half that treasure to the church. The pastor will know who needs help. Take the other half down to the docks and throw it into the water. You may keep what floats."

At that, the young man woke up and tried to forget that preposterous dream.

Two weeks later his father died. The next day his mother died. After they were buried, the young man went back to his sad, broken-down hut. He felt like a fool, but he got down on the floor and peered under the bed.

Was there... ? He couldn't tell. He found a stick and prodded the shadows.

There *was* something, something hard, under that bed.

He reached into the darkness and pulled a splintery old box out from under the bed. It certainly did not look like a treasure chest!

Slowly, he opened the lid, and inside there *was* treasure! Coins, jewelry, silver candlesticks, some silver watches, and many large gold nuggets.

He closed the box and remembered the words in the dream: "Give half that treasure to the church."

But *he* needed so many things. He could buy clothes and food, a new house, boat, and a farm. With this much treasure, he could even get married if he wanted.

Then he shook his head. Half the treasure would be more than he had ever hoped for.

He gave half the treasure to the pastor, who did not seem the least surprised by the gift. The young man then remembered the words of the dream.

"Take the other half to the dock and throw it in the water."

He walked slowly to the dock and opened the box. Half the treasure was still a lot of treasure. He could still buy some clothes, some food. He could even fix up his hut and maybe buy a boat and a new farm.

Then he remembered what else the dream had said.

"You may keep what floats."

Maybe some of it would float. Slowly he poured the coins, the gold, the jewelry, the silver into the water. Each piece fell with a single splash.

Three pieces of paper floated to the surface. It was just three shilling notes. That was such a small amount of money.

Three shillings? That was all? What could he do with three shillings?

Then that young man began to laugh. He could put those three shillings into his pocket. He'd never had three shillings in his pocket before. With those three shillings, he could leave the village where he thought the townspeople had whispered, "Oh, that poor young man. Isn't he the son of a thief?"

He could go somewhere new, do something different. With three shillings in his pocket he could do ANYTHING!

So, he left the village and walked all day. Finally, long after dark, he came to a large house in the forest. He knocked and asked the man who opened the door for a place to sleep.

"It looks to me like you might also want something to eat," the homeowner said.

The starving young cottager quickly said, "I *am* hungry, but I couldn't pay you very much."

"Don't worry about that – it is my job to feed people," said the man.

Rather soon the young man was sitting in the nicest chair he had ever sat in, eating the best bread and cheese he had ever tasted. He had never felt so comfortable.

Then, the most amazing animal interrupted his meal. It was smaller than the dogs back in his village and had much softer, fluffier fur. The fur was striped grey, white, and black. Its ears stood up like triangles, its eyes were big and green, and it had wonderful whiskers.

"What is this?" the young man asked as the animal hopped into his lap and extended one paw to slide a piece of cheese from the table.

"That's a kitten," his host told him. "He's very friendly. Just rub his head between his ears."

The kitten began to make the most amazing rumbling noise and rub his head against the side of the young man's hand. "What's he doing?" the young man asked.

"He's purring. That means he likes you."

Soon the kitten curled up on the young man's lap and went to sleep. The young man then realized that there were several more kittens in the room, hidden in the shadows, each one as adorable as the first. "What do you do with these kittens?" he asked.

"We sell them," his host said. "They are very useful to have around farms."

"Do you think you . . . I mean, could I . . . how much do they cost? I don't have much money, but I have some."

Carefully, so as not to wake the kitten, the young man pulled his three shillings out of his pocket.

The host smiled and asked, "Three shillings?" He paused a moment. "That is the exact price of a kitten."

The young man gave his host the money without even stopping to think that he had become just as poor as he had ever been. He thought that he really wasn't *truly* poor as now he had a kitten.

The next morning, the host pointed the young man in the direction of the king's castle. "He's a good king and he is always willing to hire hard workers."

The guards at the gate welcomed the young man. One of them told him to go into the great hall, where the king was in the habit of feeding all comers.

The young man took a seat in the great hall, on the other side away from the king. To his surprise, the princess came and sat right next to him. She even spoke to him. After a while, the servants brought out platters, piles, and plates of food.

Suddenly a great flood of horrible little creatures with beady black eyes, long naked tails, and pointed claws poured out of the holes in the walls. The guests screamed and shouted. They began swatting at the little beasts which were now all over the tables, gnawing at the food.

The kitten, still hiding in the young man's shirt, woke up. It leapt out of the shirt and went into action. Pounce! He was on one of the creatures. Snap! He broke its neck and tossed it aside.

Pounce!

Snap!

Pounce!

Snap!

The kitten kept killing the creatures until those that were still alive ran away screeching in terror. Then the kitten walked back to the young man, his tail high with pride.

The hall was suddenly incredibly quiet. The cottager looked up from his kitten and found himself right in front of the king.

"And what," the king asked, pointing, "is that?"

"It's a kitten. The man who sold it to me said they are particularly useful around farms."

"Young man, your kitten has saved us from a terrible plague, and you deserve a great reward. Would you like half my kingdom?"

The young man looked at the charming girl who had been sitting beside him. She smiled at him and gave a nod.

He said to the king, "Sir, I know nothing about running half a kingdom, but perhaps with your daughter at my side, we might just be able to do a good enough job?"

So that is what happened. As for the cottager and the princess, the kingdom and that cat? They all lived happily ever after.

FIFTEEN POUNDS
OF
MUSCLE AND BOUNCE

THE PRINCESS WAS SMART AND BEAUTIFUL.
Her father's kingdom was very rich.
And, since she was an only child, the law
was that the man who married her would rule the
kingdom. So, as you can imagine, that man would
need to pass a difficult test. That was just the way it
was back in the days of this story.

The King owned fifty European Hares. Not cute
little cottontail rabbits. Not long-eared jackrabbits, but
European Hares – and each European Hare is fifteen
pounds of muscle and bounce. The King, the Queen,
and the Princess all agreed that the successful candi-
date would be the one who followed those fifty hares
into the forest at dawn and then returned at sunset
with all fifty hares. Anybody who tried and failed
would have to give the King three handfuls of gold.

The sons of kings came from miles around. Each
one of them went home without their gold. The sons

of nobles appeared. They, too, went home without their gold. As did the sons of rich landowners. The sons of merchants failed and paid.

Three brothers, Per, Paul, and Jesper decided to try to win the Princess, even though they were only the sons of a farmer. Their father had told them, "I only have six handfuls of gold, so one of you better do this right."

"I will," Per said. "I'll go first because I am the oldest."

His mother made him a nice lunch. She even gave him a piece of bone-in ham. Per went to the castle. He signed the papers saying that he understood the price he would pay.

At dawn, the King released his hares. Each one ran away in a different direction. As far as Per could tell, many of them went in three directions at once. He looked for those hares all morning. Finally, he sat down to eat his lunch. As he unwrapped the ham, an old woman came tottering along the path.

"That ham smells mighty good," she said. "May I have a bite?"

"NO! This has been the worst day of my whole life. I have lost all the King's hares; I will not marry the Princess and I am losing three handfuls of gold. Do you know how much that hurts? I am not sharing my lunch with you or anyone else!"

"That's just fine," the old woman said as she tottered away.

The next day, Paul went to the castle. He also had ham in his lunch and he also lost the hares. He refused to share his ham with the old woman and came home without any gold.

Then it was Jesper's turn.

"I don't have any more gold," his father told him.

"Forget about it," his brothers said.

"What's the King going to do, tear strips off my back?" Jesper asked. The next morning, when the King released the hares, they all ran off in different directions. Jesper searched all morning and finally sat down to eat his lunch.

The old woman came tottering along the path. "May I have a bite of your ham?"

Jesper sighed. "This is the worst day of my life. I have lost the hares, I am not going to marry the princess, I don't know, maybe the King will tear strips off my back. I do know that my brothers will laugh at me." He handed his lunch to the old woman. "Here, take the whole thing. I am not very hungry, but it looks like you are."

The old woman chewed all the ham from the bone. Then she chewed the bone, first one end and then the other. She nudged Jesper, who was not paying attention.

"Watch this." She put one end of the bone in her mouth and it played a pretty tune. Every single one of those hares showed up and sat down in front of the old woman. She turned the bone around and blew into the other end. The whistle squawked and every single one of the hares bounced away.

She turned the bone around and called the hares back. Then she blew into the other end and the hares scattered. She handed the bone to Jesper. "You try."

He played a tune on the bone. It worked!

"May I keep this?" he asked.

The old woman nodded and walked away.

Just before sunset, Jesper played the calling-tune on the bone and led all fifty hares back to the castle. The King, the Queen, and the Princess all looked at each other and shook their heads.

"Excuse me, lad," the King said to Jesper. "This is most unusual. I am going to have to ask you to do it again."

"Sure," Jesper said.

The next morning the hares were released. Jesper went into the forest, played the calling tune and they all showed up. While he had them together, a young woman came down the path.

"Hares!" she said. "I love hares. May I have one?" She smiled up at him. "Please?"

"You will need to pay," he told her. "Give me a kiss."

"Give you a kiss? Eww, you're just a farm boy!"

"Do you want the hare or not?"

She decided a kiss was not so bad. She walked up to him, held her breath, and gave him a quick kiss right on the chin. Then she snatched up a hare and ran away.

Jesper was not worried. When he played the tune to call the hares that evening, all fifty showed up, even the one the girl had taken.

When the King saw all the hares, he said, "Lad, I think we need you to do this again."

Jesper said, "Sure."

The next morning, a beautiful and dignified woman asked him for a hare.

"You will need to pay," he told her. "Kiss the hare right beneath its tail."

"Kiss it *where*? That's disgusting!"

"Do you want the hare or not?"

So, she kissed that hare, right beneath its tail.

He gave her a hare, but that evening, when he called them back, all fifty showed up. He returned to the castle.

The King and the Princess looked from the hares to the Queen and frowned.

"One more time," the King told Jesper.

The next morning, a knight on horseback asked for a hare.

"Sure," Jesper said. "But you will have to pay. Kiss your horse under its tail."

"Kiss it *where*? That's rude!"

"Do you want the hare or not?"

So, the knight kissed his horse, right under its tail.

When it came time to go back to the castle, Jesper played the tune on the bone. All fifty hares returned.

That evening, the Queen and the Princess looked from the hares to the King and frowned.

The King said, "Very well, lad. One more test." He called for a large kettle. "Fill that kettle with truth if you want to win this challenge."

"Very well," Jesper said. "The second time I took the hares out a delightful girl asked me for one. I told her she could earn it with a kiss and –"

"That's enough," the Princess quickly said. "The kettle is already one-third full."

"The next day, an elegant woman asked me for a hare. I told her she could earn it by kissing it under its talil and –"

"That's enough," the Queen interrupted. "The kettle is already two-thirds full."

"This morning, a knight on horseback asked me for a hare. I told him he could pay for it by kissing his horse under its tail and then . . ."

"That is enough," the King said. "The kettle is overflowing. Now it is up to the Princess to make a choice about you."

But nobody knows if the Princess and Jesper lived happily ever after.

However, he did get some of the King's gold to give to his father.

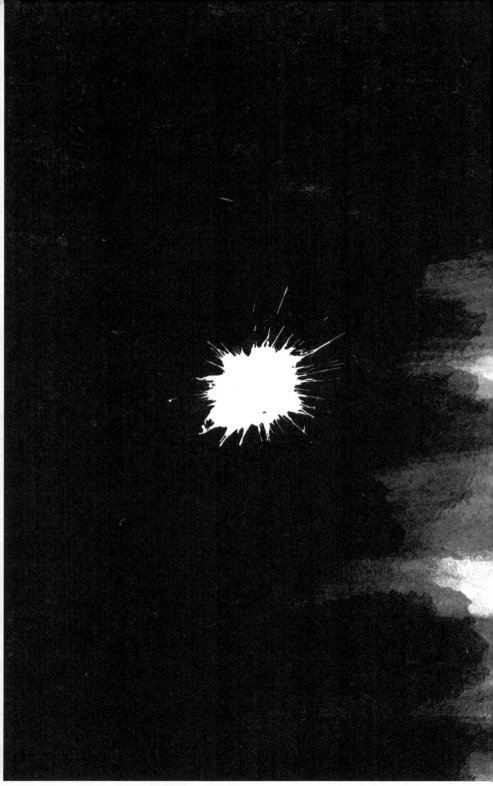

ANGRY NISSE
IS
NO JOKE

THE DAIRY MAID KNEW ALL ABOUT THE NISSE, the little man who lived in the barn. Like all Nissen, he was the size of a child, wore a pointed red cap, and dressed in a grey vest and trousers.

Nissen were fiercely loyal, not so much to the people of the farm, but to the cattle and horses and to the buildings. She'd never seen the Nisse, and that was a good thing.

All Nissen loved to play tricks on people and she didn't want the Nisse in her barn, sneaking up to twist the cows' tails as she was trying to milk them. A tricky Nisse was a problem. An angry Nisse was even worse. And the best way to anger a Nisse was to fail to give him his Christmas porridge.

It was Christmas Eve, but the dairy maid was not thinking about the Nisse. Cook had been cooking for days and a cooking Cook meant a running dairy maid. The maid ran from kitchen to dairy and dairy to kitchen for milk, cream, sweet butter, thick cream, sour milk, salted butter, and clotted cream.

Finally, long after sunset, Cook took off her apron and threw in the corner. "I am done."

But, before the dairy maid could limp away, Cook handed the maid a beautiful bowl filled with porridge. It was a white-rice porridge made with cream, butter, sugar, and cinnamon.

Cook told her, "Take this to the Nisse. When you come back you can have your own porridge."

As the dairy maid trudged down the path to the barn, her feet scuffing the packed snow, she stared down at the beautiful porridge in the beautiful bowl. Never in her life had she tasted white rice porridge. What was it like?

She sat on a rickety old bench outside the barn. Surely the Nisse wouldn't miss a little taste of the cream Cook had poured over the rice.

Oh-so-carefully, the dairy maid scooped up just a tiny bite. The cream and the cinnamon tasted like Christmas, but she stared in dismay at the porridge. The tip of the spoon had left a mark in the cream. The Nisse would know what she had done!

He would be furious! He might even bring his Nisse friends to the barn where they would all hide in the loft and make it impossible to pull down hay for the cows.

She tried oh-so-hard to smooth the surface of the cream, but only smeared the pattern Cook had made with the cinnamon. She licked the cream from the spoon and tried again. This time she messed up the butter. She licked the spoon again. Everything she tried made the bowl of white rice porridge with cream, butter, sugar and cinnamon look worse.

What could she do? She'd ruined the Nisse's porridge. She wouldn't even get her own porridge when Cook found out what she'd done.

"Then why don't I eat the whole thing?" she asked herself. "The Nisse is important, but so am I. I milked the cows, separated the cream, churned the butter, and fetched everything Cook needed. All I get is every-day oat porridge with milk so thin it's blue?"

Defiantly, she scooped up every bit of the porridge. The cream, butter, sugar, and cinnamon filled her stomach with joy. The bowl was empty, and she couldn't give the Nisse an empty bowl! She tiptoed back to the kitchen and peeked in the door.

Cook was nowhere to be seen. Quickly, she went to the stove and spooned her oat porridge into his bowl. She thought, "Let the Nisse have the thin, blue milk for a change!"

She scampered out of the kitchen and back to the barn. She put the bowl on the small table for the Nisse and turned to run away.

She heard his voice before she reached the door: "What is this garbage?"

She stopped and answered, "Your Christmas porridge."

"This is not my Christmas porridge," the Nisse snapped.

Slowly she turned around and looked at the Nisse. "No, it's not," she said.

"Did *you* eat my porridge?"

She was still angry enough to answer with the truth. "Yes. I was exhausted and I have been working for days. I was hungry. It is Christmas Eve and all Cook was going to give me was my ordinary porridge. I wanted something special for myself."

He glared at her. "How do you plan to pay for eating my porridge?"

"I need to pay?"

He nodded. "Indeed, you do."

She looked at him. "What if I danced with you?"

He thought a bit and said, "Can you dance the Swedish *Hambo*?"

"Don't be silly," she replied. "This is Norway,"

"If you learn the Swedish *Hambo*, we're even," he said.

"Very well," she answered.

The Nisse put his hands on her shoulders. She heard music inside her head. He twirled her around, faster and faster. "ONE two THREE!" he shouted. "LEFT, turn, RIGHT. BEND YOUR KNEE, pivot on your toe during that turn."

It was much harder than it sounded. The dairy maid's feet tangled but the Nisse whirled her faster.

"Slow down," she cried as her skirt twisted and billowed around her.

"You're the girl who stole a Nisse's porridge," he told her. "You can do this."

And he whirled her around, chanting:

"My porridge you did take,
You can't dance, you must fake."

The dairy maid's feet began to figure out what they were supposed to do. Her anger dissolved into giggles.

The Nisse giggled with her until everything went dark. She collapsed on the floor, her head still spinning. The cowman found her the next morning, collapsed next to the untouched bowl of oat porridge.

She had a smile on her face, one that never quite went away, even after she went back to being just the dairy maid. Sometimes, when she tripped slightly while carrying buckets of milk to the dairy, she thought that she could feel the Nisse steadying her.

And, every Christmas, she told Cook that she wanted a bowl of white rice porridge with cream, butter, sugar, and cinnamon, just like the one Cook made for the Nisse.

MAKE
THE
KIDHAUS
PAY

THERE WAS ONCE AN OLD WOMAN WHO HAD A most unusual spindle-whorl. Although she was very poor, the whorl was made of pure gold. One day, as she was sitting outside her hut spinning, the golden whorl fell to the ground and rolled away, down the hill.

The old woman dropped her spindle and ran after the whorl, but she couldn't catch it. It rolled and rolled, right into the mound at the bottom of the hill.

One of the hidden folks lived in the mound. His name was Kidhaus.

The old woman went crying to her husband. "Kidhaus has stolen my golden spindle-whorl. Go tell him I want it back."

The old man picked up his cudgel, walked down the hill and climbed to the top of the mound.

"Give!" he shouted. WHACK went the heavy stick on the top of the mound.

"Back!" WHACK!

"The!" WHACK!

"Spindle!" WHACK!

"Whorl!" WHACK!

"I don't have a spindle-whorl," Kidhaus shouted from inside the mound.

"My wife has no spindle-whorl and you must pay," said the angry man.

"Will you take a cow that gives twenty-eight pounds of milk a day?" came the shout from below the ground.

That was a lot of milk. The man responded, "Yes."

"Very good. You have a cow," said the voice.

When the old man went home he found that he did indeed have a cow, one that gave twenty-eight pounds of milk a day.

The old woman wasn't happy about losing the golden spindle-whorl, but making butter and cheese out of all that milk kept her busy. One day she said to herself, "If only we had some oats, I could make porridge with all this milk."

When her husband came home, she said, "That Kidhaus still has my golden spindle-whorl and he must give it back. If he won't, make him give us a barrel of oats."

Once more, the old man picked up his cudgel, walked down the hill, and climbed to the top of the mound.

"Give!" WHACK!

"Back!" WHACK!

"The!" WHACK!

"Spindle!" WHACK!

"Whorl!" WHACK!

"I do not have a spindle-whorl!" Kidhaus shouted.

"Then you must pay, for the golden spindle-whorl is gone."

"What do you want?"

"A barrel of oatmeal."

"Very good. You have a barrel of oatmeal."

The old woman wasn't happy about losing her golden spindle-whorl, but making and eating all that porridge kept her busy.

One day she and the old man decided they would not, indeed *could not*, eat another bite of porridge.

"But what can we do with it?" the old man asked.

"We can take it up to heaven and give it to the angels," his wife answered.

He asked, "How are we going to get to heaven?"

"With a ladder," she said, matter-of-factly.

The old man thought for a bit and said, "We don't have a ladder long enough to reach heaven."

"The Kidhaus still has my golden spindle-whorl and he must give it back. If he won't, he must give us a ladder tall enough to reach heaven."

The old man picked up his cudgel, walked down the hill and climbed to the top of the mound.

"Give!" WHACK!

"Back!" WHACK!

"The!" WHACK!

"Spin—"

The Kidhaus completely lost his patience and screamed,

"I DID NOT TAKE YOUR WIFE'S GOLDEN SPINDLE-WHORL.

I DO NOT HAVE YOUR WIFE'S GOLDEN SPINDLE-WHORL.

I CANNOT GIVE YOUR WIFE'S GOLDEN SPINDLE-WHORL BACK AND I DON'T WANT TO HEAR ANYMORE ABOUT YOUR WIFE'S GOLDEN SPINDLE-WHORL."

"Then you must pay, for the golden spindle-whorl is gone," retorted the man.

The Kidhaus asked, "Well, what do you want?"

"A ladder tall enough to reach heaven," said the old man, matter-of-factly.

A muffled laugh came from below the ground. The voice said, "This I've got to see. Very well. You have a new ladder."

The old man returned home and there was the ladder. He and his wife set the ladder up in the rocky field below their house. They cooked all the rest of the porridge and put it in the biggest kettle they could find. Then, slowly and carefully, side-by-side on the ladder, holding the kettle between them, they climbed... and climbed... and climbed... and climbed.

Every time they looked down, the ground was farther away. Every time they looked up, they were

closer and closer to heaven. The ladder swayed. The old man swayed. The old woman swayed and...

CRASH! The old man fell on the rocks.

CRASH-SPLAT! The old woman fell on the rocks.

RATTLE-CRASH-SPLAT! The kettle full of porridge fell on the rocks.

To this very day, the people in the southern part of Iceland near those rocks where the ladder was placed, say that the orange and white lichen on the rocks is the remains of the porridge. Some of them even say that the white parts of the lichen are what is left of the old folks' brains.

Such is what happens when you make the Kidhaus pay.

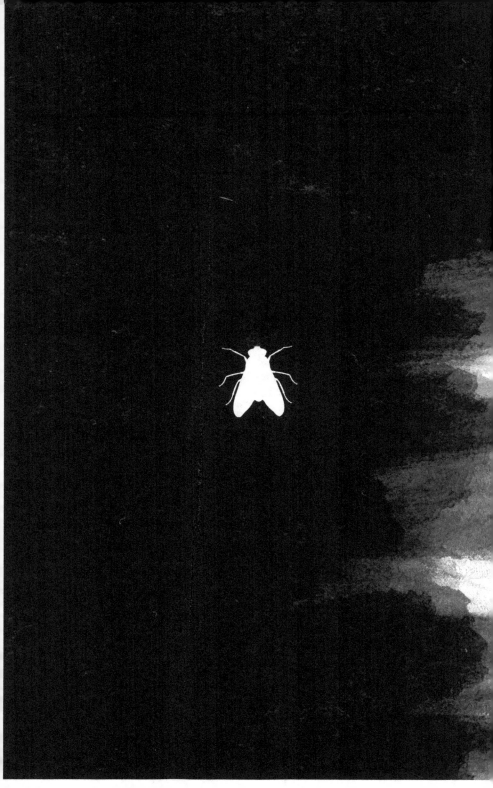

TRUE STORY
OF
THOR'S HAMMER

PART ONE: THOR NEEDS A HAMMER

THE NORSE GOD THOR HAD ONLY ONE JOB, and that job was to kill giants. Every chance he got, Thor went out and killed giants, but it was not enough. There were too many giants. They all wanted to fight Thor because his father, the god Ódinn, had killed the first giant, the one named Ymir.

"I need," Thor shouted, "something better than my sword and my fists. I need a REAL weapon, a weapon worthy of my strength, my muscles, and my bright red hair."

The very next morning, Thor woke up and rolled over to give his wife a kiss. But something was really wrong. "Sif, what happened to your hair?"

Sif opened her eyes. "My hair!" She put her hand to her head and screamed, "It's gone!"

She threw herself out of bed, burst into tears, and ran out of the room. She was probably going to find a weapon.

Thor shouted for Loki, his brother. When the Trickster did not appear, Thor went looking and when he found him, he wrapped his huge hand around the back of Loki's neck and lifted him off his feet. "What did you do to Sif's hair?"

"Sif's hair?" Loki squeaked. "Is there something wrong with Sif's hair?"

"It's gone."

"Gone? Do you mean she doesn't have any hair? I bet she looks cute without any hair."

Thor's hand tightened on Loki's neck. "Don't you be calling my wife cute. I want her hair back on her head, and I want it back today."

With that, he dropped the Trickster on the floor.

"Alright," Loki said. "Some people just can't take a joke. I know some dwarves – I can fix this." He scampered away to find the dwarves known as the sons of Ivaldi.

After he had flattered the dwarves into agreeing to do the job by telling them they were the very best dwarves, the oldest son began making a marvelous golden ship, one that could sail over the seas and through the air.

"I said to make for Sif a head of golden hair," Loki complained.

The second dwarf nodded. "We're not making a gift for Thor without making a gift for your father, Óðinn."

"He needs a spear," the third dwarf interrupted. "For that other god, Freyr, we should make a ship that sails through the air!"

Finally, the sons of Ivaldi gave Loki the ship, the spear, and a great braid of shining golden hair.

"It can't be just a wig," Loki said.

"It's not," the first dwarf responded. "She puts that on her head and it stays there. It grows there. It's just like real hair but it's also real gold. She will be pleased and so will Thor. That's what we want."

Loki took the gifts and left the sons of Ivaldi. Halfway back to Asgard, the fortress where all the gods, known as the Æsir, live, he had an idea. At once he turned and went to the forge and spoke to a pair of dwarves who had no names.

"Look at the gifts the sons of Ivaldi made for Freyr, Óðinn, and Thor," he said. "Ivaldi's sons are very good dwarves, but I think you might be better."

The dwarves examined the ship, the spear, and the hair. "Right," one of them said. "We can do better than this."

"Prove it," Loki challenged. "Make gifts the Æsir like better than these, and you win."

"What do we win?"

"My head," Loki said. "If the Æsir like the gifts you made better than these, you can have my head."

"Sounds good to us." The dwarves set about preparing their tools and heating up their forge.

Loki immediately turned himself into a fly. As the dwarves worked on a golden boar for Freyr, Loki bit the one who was pumping the bellows, but the dwarf ignored the pain.

As they worked on the arm rings for Óðinn, Fly Loki bit again, but the dwarf did not even try to brush him away. Finally, as the dwarves made a great war hammer for Thor, Loki bit the dwarf's eyebrow so hard that the dwarf had to brush the blood out of his eye.

When the dwarf took his hand away from the bellows, the fire in the forge flickered slightly and Thor's hammer emerged with a somewhat short handle.

"Well then," Loki said, quickly changing back into his own shape. "Let's go see what the Æsir have to say about these gifts."

Óðinn liked the arm ring better than the spear. The spear could kill an entire army, but the gold arm ring dripped out more gold arm rings every nine days. Óðinn was a god who liked his gold.

Freyr liked the boar better than the ship, and Thor was delighted by the hammer.

"Your head is ours," the dwarves shouted at Loki.

"Wait," he cried. "Thor, didn't you notice? That hammer is not perfect, it has a short handle."

"It's perfect for me! It will fly all the better the way it is."

"Now, your head is ours," the dwarves shouted. One of them pulled out his knife and held it to Loki's throat.

"Stop," Loki cried out. "You are cutting my throat. I didn't promise you my throat, I promised you my head."

And, since the dwarves could not figure out how to remove Loki's head without cutting his throat, that's how Loki kept his head.

PART TWO: THE HAMMER VANISHES

That hammer of Thor's was indeed perfect. He killed giant after giant until he woke up one morning, reached for his hammer, and found it gone. "Loki! Get in here."

Loki flickered into the room. "What's wrong?"

"My hammer! What have you done with my hammer?"

"N-nothing."

Even though he was furious, Thor knew that the Trickster was not to blame. But he couldn't help yelling: "Then what happened to it?!"

"I don't know."

Thor did not believe him. "You don't know? What kind of a trickster are you?"

"I can find it, really I can," Loki said quickly. "I will borrow Freya's falcon-feathered flight suit."

"Freya is not speaking to you. *None* of the goddesses are speaking to you, not after you managed to insult each and every one of them during the last party. She won't lend you her falcon-feathered flight suit."

"Yes, she will," Loki insisted. "I was just fooling around at the party. She knows the difference between fooling around and danger. But if she won't give the suit? What if we don't find the hammer? What if the giants figure out that you don't have it? What if one of the giants *has* your hammer? What's going to happen then, Thor?"

"Alright, ask Freya. But I'm coming along. I'll try to protect you if she's still too mad to listen."

Freya did know the difference between a joke, even a bad one, and real danger. As soon as she heard that Thor's hammer was missing, she gave Loki the falcon-feathered flight suit.

The Trickster vanished, then almost at once he flickered, like a flame, back into view.

"I found it." He looked sideways at Freya. "I even know how to get it back. But --"

"But what?" Freya asked.

"A giant named Thrym has the hammer. He is willing to return it, but there will be a price," said Loki.

"And that price is?" Freya asked.

Loki put up both hands in a gesture of surrender. "Hey, don't blame me for this news. I am just the messenger. The giant wants you as his wife."

"Do not tell me you are trying to do this again!" Freya said through clenched teeth. "You once before tried to give me to that Builder fellow, to pay for the wall he built around Asgard. Now you want me to marry Thrym the giant?"

"But Freya, I need my hammer back," Thor said.

"Get those dwarves to make you another one!"

"Those dwarves aren't speaking to Loki," replied Thor.

"And neither am I, after this. I am not marrying a giant!" Freya shouted so loudly that the famous necklace she always wore burst apart, sending a shower of links about Asgard and to the planets below.

PART THREE: A PLAN FOR THE WEDDING.

"Wait," Loki said. "Let's try to fool Thrym."

"How?" Thor and Freya both asked at the same time.

"We put Thor in a wedding dress and -- "

"No," Thor bellowed. "I am not marrying a giant!"

At the same time, Freya started to laugh. "You can do it, Thor. I'll even make the dress."

"You don't have to marry the giant," Loki said. "You just have to pretend."

Thor thought for a moment and then said, "What are people going to say about me if I put on a wedding dress? That would be unacceptable for me to do."

"They will say you are a fine, brave Thunder God," Freya said in her sweetest voice. "You need the hammer. *We* need you to have the hammer. This marriage to a giant is such a little thing. Nobody even needs to know about it."

Finally, the two of them, Loki with tricks and Freya with sweetness, convinced Thor. Loki flashed back to Thrym's cave to tell him his offer had been accepted. Freya and her maids began cutting and sewing.

When the big day came, Freya and Loki stuffed Thor into his embroidered dress. They draped him with most of Freya's jewels and wrapped him in a heavy veil.

"What if somebody sees me?" he grumbled. "I won't be 'Thundering Thor' anymore. I'll just be 'Thor the Fool.'"

"This is not a story that will ever be told," Freya soothed him while Loki just grinned and wriggled into his maid-servant's dress.

The trickster harnessed Thor's goats to a small wagon, and off they went, bride and maid, to Thrym's cave.

PART FOUR: THE WEDDING DAY ARRIVES

Thrym and his entire family had been working for days to prepare the wedding feast. As soon as Thor and

Loki arrived, Thor gobbled up three whole salmon and a roasted calf and ate them all in a mighty swallow.

"My," Thrym said. "I do not think I have ever seen a bride with an appetite like that."

"Freya is so nervous and eager to be your wife that she hasn't eaten for eight days," Loki explained while Thor drank three barrels of cider and ale.

"And I certainly have not seen a bride who *drinks* like that," Thrym said.

"Freya is so nervous and eager to be your wife that she has had nothing to drink for eight days," Loki said.

Thrym decided he would steal a kiss from his bride before the actual ceremony. But when he lifted the veil, Thor glared at him so fiercely that he backed away. "I have never seen a bride whose eyes burn like coals."

Loki nodded. "Freya is so nervous and eager to be your wife that she has not slept for eight days."

"Well then, it is time for the wedding," Thrym shouted. "Bring out Thor's hammer so that Freya and I may lay our hands on it as we exchange vows."

The giants brought the Hammer up from deep in the mountain where Thrym had hidden it. Loki kept his hand on Thor's shoulder to silence him as the giants put the Hammer in his lap. Then, Loki whispered, "Go."

Thor stood up. His mighty shoulders burst through the seams of the wedding dress as he lifted his hammer over his head. It was time for Thor and his hammer to bring destruction to the giants who had always been, would always *be,* enemies of the gods.

Loki laughed the whole time while Thor chased the giants. He was annoying that way. He knew this marriage story was too good not to tell, especially since he would tell it to everyone. That's why everybody knows about the time Thor was tricked into wearing a wedding dress to fool the giants!

PART FIVE: THOR SEEKS OUT A KETTLE

When he wasn't being married off to a giant, Thor was a god with a single job – to kill giants with that hammer of his. But sometimes he found other ways to deal with a giant or two, without using the hammer.

The Norse gods, the Æsir, decided to have a party. Not just any party, but a spectacular party. And, for a spectacular party, the Æsir needed vast quantities of things to drink. They needed to brew those quantities in a giant kettle.

But nobody in Asgard had a kettle.

"Try Ægir," Loki suggested. "He's the god of the sea, he should have some giant kettles."

So Thor, along with his god-of-war brother Tyr, went to talk to Ægir, who was sitting armpit-deep in the cold surf of the northern waters.

"We're having a party," Tyr began.

"You are? I don't suppose you are thinking of inviting me."

"Umm -- " Thor said. The god of the sea wasn't known to be much fun at parties.

Tyr swallowed. "Actually, we were hoping to borrow one of your kettles, one for brewing vast quantities of ale."

Ægir, sea foam dripping from his beard, glared at Tyr. "Doesn't that foster-father of yours have the most enormous of all kettles?"

Tyr nodded.

"Go ask him," grunted Ægir.

"But -- " Tyr swallowed again. "Hymir is a giant and my foster-father but that doesn't mean he likes me. He took me in as part of a treaty he made with my father Óðinn, but the treaty didn't work out."

"That is not my problem." Ægir turned and flopped back into the water like a huge fish, splashing freezing sea foam all over both Tyr and Thor.

"I guess I'll go talk to Hymir," Tyr said.

Thor dried his hammer. "I'll come along."

Tyr shook his head. "That is not a good idea. It's not really my foster-father who has the problem with me. It's his mother who hates me. She has nine hundred heads. A battle will start as soon as one of those heads sees you and that hammer."

"She won't know it's me. I'll disguise myself as a little boy. And I promise I won't use my hammer at all."

Tyr managed a smile. "That would almost be worth seeing."

"Here you go," Thor's bright-red hair became soft and silky, his great beard vanished, and his shoulders, waist, and legs became strangely delicate. His great hammer seemed to be nothing more than a child's toy, tucked in his belt.

When Tyr and Thor reached Hymir's Hall, the 900-headed grandmother glared at them with every single one of her eyes.

"Who's that?" she asked Tyr.

"It's just a boy," he told her.

"Never known you to have kids following the god of war around," she scoffed.

"He's not following me around." But before Tyr could think of a way to explain Thor to his grandmother, his foster-mother told them to come in.

"Your father will be home soon," she told Tyr. "He's even crankier than he used to be, so I'm going to put you up on the roof beam where we store the kettles. That will give me a chance to calm him down before he sees you."

So, Tyr and Thor hid among the vast kettles stored upside down on the beams. When Hymir walked in from the ice and cold, he immediately stopped and glared up at the beam.

"Who's that you have hidden up there?" he asked his wife.

"Your foster-son Tyr, and his young friend. You must remember that even giants treat their guests nicely." As she spoke, she handed Hymir a towel so he could dry the melting icicles in his beard.

Hymir glared at the beam and shrugged with such force that his glare and shrug brought Tyr, Thor, and all but the largest kettle crashing to the floor.

Hymir looked at his guests and said to the servants, "Alright, let's eat. We need three oxen for dinner. There's one for Tyr, one for me, and we can split the third with my mother. The kid won't need anything more than scraps."

However, when the servants arrived with the food and brought in the oxen, Thor immediately ate two of them, leaving Tyr, Hymir, and his mother to split the third.

"If you are going to eat like that," Hymir said, "we will have to go fishing tomorrow."

"I hate fishing. I'm not fishing with you," Tyr told his foster-father.

"But I will go with you," tiny Thor said.

"You'll have to bring your own bait, child," Hymir warned him.

The next morning, Thor killed Hymir's best ox and dragged the head to the boat to be used as bait. He took over the boat and rowed much farther out to sea than Hymir expected.

"I think we'd better stop here," the giant finally said. He put his own bait on a hook and dropped it deep into the water. Almost at once, he pulled up two whales. "Think you can do better than that, child?"

Thor looked into the water and then dropped his hook directly into the mouth of Jörmungandr, the terrible serpent, and the son of Loki. The serpent circled around the entire planet by biting his own tail. It was enormous, as you can imagine.

With the bait now in his mouth, the serpent let go of his own tail and swallowed down the ox head.

"I've got something," Thor shouted, pulling on his line. The serpent fought back. Thor stood up in the boat and pulled harder, so hard that his feet broke through the bottom of the boat.

"Careful," Hymir squealed in a high and terrified voice.

At that moment, Thor grew back to his full size. He planted his feet on the bottom of the sea and kept pulling until Jörmungandr's head emerged from the water and rested on the side of the boat.

"No, you can't have that serpent!" Hymir cried out. He pulled out his belt knife and cut the fishing line, allowing the serpent to escape.

"What did you do that for?" Thor pushed Hymir so hard that the giant fell into the water. Thor then picked up the boat, whales and all, and waded to shore, with Hymir swimming unhappily at his side.

Thor yelled at Hymir as he swam by his side. "You cut loose my fishing catch. You must pay for that!"

When they got to shore, Hymir said, "Well then, you can have my largest kettle as payment. Take it."

After they arrived back at the great hall, Thor picked up the kettle and walked quickly out of the hall with Tyr right behind him.

Tyr said to Thor, "You do know I'm never going to be able to go back there after everything that just happened?"

Thor laughed. "Why would you want to? We have the kettle that we came for!"

And that's the time Thor solved a problem without using his hammer.

GOTTA GET
UP THE
DOVREFJELL!

THERE WAS ONCE A HEN WHO LIVED NEAR THE
Dovrefjell, a mountain range in Norway.
The story of Hen is rather creepy.

One morning this hen woke up, jumped out of
the oak tree where she slept, and started running. And
as she ran, she said, "Gotta get up the Dovrefell, gotta
get up the Dovrefjell."

Hen ran so hard, Hen ran so fast, that she
smacked right into the rooster.

Rooster asked, "What is up with you? What is up
with you?"

And Hen said, "Gotta get up the Dovrefjell, gotta
get up the Dovrefjell."

Rooster decided to go up the Dovrefjell with Hen.
The two of them ran so hard and so fast that Rooster
smacked right into the duck.

Duck asked, "Ack, ack, why the whack?"

Rooster answered, "Ask Hen.

And Hen said, "Gotta get up the Dovrefjell, gotta get up the Dovrefjell."

Duck decided to go up the Dovrefjell with Hen and Rooster. The three of them ran so hard and so fast that Duck smacked right into the goose.

Goose asked, "Onk, onk, why the bonk?"

Duck answered, "Ask Rooster."

Rooster answered, "Ask Hen."

And Hen said, "Gotta get up the Dovrefjell, gotta get up the Dovrefjell."

Goose decided to go up the Dovrefjell with Hen and Rooster and Duck. The four of them ran so hard and so fast that Goose smacked right into Fox.

Fox slyly said, "My goodness! What have we here?"

Goose answered, "Ask Duck."

Duck answered, "Ask Rooster."

Rooster answered, "Ask Hen."

And Hen said, "Gotta get up the Dovrefjell, gotta get up the Dovrefjell."

Fox said, "Listen, folks – I've been watching you travel about. You've been running around all day. There's no way you are going to get up the Dovrefjell before sunset. Why don't you all come to my den? You can get a good night's sleep and leave early in the morning. That way it'll be easy to get up the Dovrefjell."

Goose said, "Yes."

Duck said, "Yes."

Rooster said, "Yes."

But Hen muttered, "Gotta get up the Dovrefjell, gotta get up the Dovrefjell."

Nevertheless, she went to Fox's den with the others.

She insisted on sleeping up next to the smoke hole, and she made Rooster perch next to her. Duck and Goose slept on the floor, beside the fire.

Early the next morning, before the sun had even started to rise, Hen woke up. Something in Fox's den smelled simply horrible! She peered down at the fire and saw Fox roasting Duck and Goose! He hadn't even taken their feathers off.

Hen nudged Rooster. "Wake up! We gotta get up, gotta get up the Dovrefjell."

The two of them wriggled out of the smoke hole and Hen started running, with Rooster right behind her.

They ran and they ran and they ran, until they finally reached the top of the Dovrefjell.

Hen collapsed in a heap. Rooster collapsed right beside her.

"We did it!" Hen shouted.

"We did," Rooster agreed, "but I have a question: *Why?* Why did we have to get up the Dovrefjell? What was so important that we lost our new friends to Fox?"

"It was because of a dream I had," Hen told Rooster. "I dreamt that the whole world would come to an end if I didn't get up the Dovrefjell. But we did it, Rooster! We saved the whole world."

The Hen was right. The world is still here, isn't it?

PRONUNCIATION GUIDE

The names do come from Old Norse, which is no longer a spoken language, although scholars have developed at least *approaches* to the actual pronunciation.

Here are my suggestions on how to say these names.

Ægir = A-geer (God)
Æsir = Ah-seer (Gods)
Freya = Froy-ah (Goddess)
Freyr = Froy-eer (God)
Ivaldi = Ih-val-dee (Dwarf)
Jesper = Yes-per (Boy)
Jórmungdander = Your-mun-gand-er (World Serpent)
Kidhaus = Kid-howse (Nisse)
Nisse = Nees-eh (Supernatural rock dweller)
Sif = Siv (Thor's wife)
Thrym = Thrihm (Giant)
Tyr = Tihr (God)
Hymir = Hi-meer (Giant)
Dovrefjell = Dove-reh-fyell (Mountain)

In the names *Thor* and Ódin, the sound written by "th" or "d" is a blend of our English "d" and "th" sounds. So it's "Dthohr" and "Ohdthin."

In all these names (and indeed in Old Norse) the accent is always on the first syllable.

ABOUT THE AUTHOR
HARRIET COLE

When Harriet was a kid, she heard her father read "The Three Billy Goats Gruff" out loud so many times that she fell in love with slightly weird folktales, especially Norwegian ones. Her interest in Norse stories expanded when she discovered the Icelandic Saga material which is sometimes beyond weird. Now, her favorite Norse stories (folktales and myths) are those that are simply weird and just scary enough to be perfect for big kids who want something more than fairytale princesses.

ABOUT THE ILLUSTRATOR
C.S. FRITZ

Casey "C.S." Fritz grew up on a farm in Oregon, where he milked cows and had a pet pig. To escape the endless chores...Casey would draw. As a teenager, Casey's family moved to Arizona. It was there beneath the fiery gaze of the Southwestern sun, that he spent most of his life. Graduating school, marrying the love of his life and having two wild kids. He now is an award-winning author and illustrator with published titles such as... *The Cottonmouth Trilogy, Good Night Tales, The Moonman Cometh, Seekers,* and *Good Night Classics!*

CPSIA information can be obtained
at www.ICGtesting.com
Printed in the USA
JSHW040505100221
11623JS00008B/141